PUFFIN BOOKS

Dinosaur Trouble

Dick King-Smith served in the Grenadier Guards during the Second World War, and afterwards spent twenty years as a farmer in Gloucestershire, the county of his birth. Many of his stories are inspired by his farming experiences. Later he taught at a village primary school. His first book, *The Fox Busters*, was published in 1978. Since then he has written a great number of children's books, including *The Sheep-Pig* (winner of the Guardian Award and filmed as *Babe*), *Harry's Mad*, *Noah's Brother*, *The Hodgeheg*, *Martin's Mice*, *Ace*, *The Cuckoo Child* and *Harriet's Hare* (winner of the Children's Book Award in 1995). At the British Book Awards in 1991 he was voted Children's Author of the Year. He has three children, a large number of grandchildren and several great-grandchildren, and lives in a seventeenth-century cottage only a crow's flight from the house where he was born.

Dinosaur Trouble

Dick King-Smith

Illustrated by Ben Cort

PUFFIN

PUFFIN BOOKS

Published by the Penguin Group
Penguin Books Ltd, 80 Strand, London WC2R 0RL, England
Penguin Group (USA) Inc., 375 Hudson Street, New York, New York 10014, USA
Penguin Group (Canada), 90 Eglinton Avenue East, Suite 700, Toronto, Ontario, Canada M4P 2Y3
(a division of Pearson Penguin Canada Inc.)
Penguin Ireland, 25 St Stephen's Green, Dublin 2, Ireland (a division of Penguin Books Ltd)
Penguin Group (Australia), 250 Camberwell Road, Camberwell, Victoria 3124, Australia
(a division of Pearson Australia Group Pty Ltd)
Penguin Books India Pvt Ltd, 11 Community Centre, Panchsheel Park, New Delhi – 110 017, India
Penguin Group (NZ), cnr Airborne and Rosedale Roads, Albany, Auckland 1310, New Zealand
(a division of Pearson New Zealand Ltd)
Penguin Books (South Africa) (Pty) Ltd, 24 Sturdee Avenue, Rosebank, Johannesburg 2196,
South Africa

Penguin Books Ltd, Registered Offices: 80 Strand, London WC2R 0RL, England

www.penguin.com

First published 2005
Published in this edition 2005

8

Text copyright © Fox Busters Ltd, 2005
Illustrations copyright © Ben Cort, 2005
All rights reserved

The moral right of the author and illustrator has been asserted

Set in 17/22.5 Perpetua
Made and printed in England by Clays Ltd, St Ives plc

British Library Cataloguing in Publication Data
A CIP catalogue record for this book is available from the British Library

ISBN-13: 978–0–14–131845–5

www.greenpenguin.co.uk

Chapter One

When he hatched from his egg, the first thing the baby saw was a huge face looking down at him. Above a long, toothless, beaked jaw two large eyes stared into his as he struggled free of the egg. Once the baby was out, he could see that the creature had big leathery wings, stretching from its fingers to its knees, and that it had long, slender, thin legs.

'Hullo!' it said.

'Who are you?' asked the baby.

'Your mother,' the creature replied.
'Nice to see you. Let's go flying,' and she
spread her big leathery wings and took off.

Could I do that, wondered the baby?

Only one way to find out. So he spread his very small wings and flew up after his mother.

'Well done!' she cried when he reached her. 'It's nice to be nidifugous, isn't it?'

'What does "nidifugous" mean, Mum?' the baby asked.

'It means to be able to fly as soon as you're hatched. All pterodactyls can.'

'What does "pterodactyl" mean, Mum?'

'Creatures like us,' the baby's mother replied. '"*Pteron*" means a wing and "*daktylos*" means a finger. Each of my wings is attached to each of my fourth fingers, see? And so are yours.'

'So I'm a whatever-you-said, am I?'

'A pterodactyl. Yes, you are, my son. And a very pulchritudinous one too.'

'What does "pulchritudinous" mean, Mum?'

'Beautiful.'

'Oh,' said the baby pterodactyl, and he kicked his little legs happily as he flew high above the rocky land.

'Now,' said his mother, 'there's the matter of nomenclature.'

'What,' said the baby, 'does "nomenclature" mean, Mum?'

'Names. You have to have one.'

'Gosh, you do know a lot of long words, Mum.'

'One has to,' said his mother, 'in these Jurassic days, if one wants to survive. Who knows, one day pterodactyls might become extinct. And before you ask me what "extinct" means, I'll tell you. It means gone, finished, kaput, dead and done for.'

'But, Mum,' the baby said, 'I don't want to be extinct.'

'Don't worry your head about it,' his mother said. 'If it should happen, it won't be for millions and millions of years, my son. Now then, what shall we call you? You ask enough questions. How about Nosy? How d'you like that?'

The baby waggled his small but rather long snout.

'I don't mind,' he said, 'but, Mum, what's your name?'

'Aviatrix,' said his mother.

'What does "aviatrix" mean, Mum?' asked Nosy.

'A female flier. In the skills of flying,

among all pterodactyls I am paramount.'

This time Nosy didn't ask anything. He simply said, 'I suppose that means "the best".'

'It does, Nosy, my boy,' replied Aviatrix. 'It most certainly does.'

Mother and son flew on, side by side. Nosy flapped along as fast as he could, while his mother flew slowly so that he could keep up with her.

'Mum,' said Nosy after a while, 'where are we going?'

'To see your father,' said Aviatrix.

'Oh. What's he called?'

'His name is Clawed. You'll see why when you meet him. Never have there been claws like his.'

Before long they left behind the dry

stony place
where Nosy
had hatched
among the
hot rocks,
and came to a
wood. Here
there were quite a
number of pterodactyls,
hanging upside down as
pterodactyls do, each gripping
a branch with its taloned feet. The
biggest one, Nosy could see as they
dropped lower, had the most enormous
claws.

'There he is!' cried Aviatrix. 'There's
my Clawed! Come on, Nosy, come and
meet your daddy!'

Chapter Two

When they landed, Aviatrix could see
that Clawed was fast asleep. She hung
herself head down at one side of him.
Nosy, copying his mother, hung himself
on the other side. He thought of saying,
'Hullo, Daddy,' but there didn't seem
much point, so he said nothing.

Then suddenly Clawed said in a loud

deep voice, 'Watch out, everybody!'

'What does Daddy mean?' asked Nosy.

'Haven't a clue,' replied his mother. 'Your father is a somniloquist.'

'What does "somniloquist" mean, Mum?'

'Someone who talks in his sleep. I expect he'll say something else in a minute,' and almost immediately Clawed shouted, 'T. rex approaching! Scramble! Scramble!'

Aviatrix raised a wing and smacked her husband across his face.

'Wake up, Clawed!' she said. 'You're dreaming.'

Clawed opened his eyes and shook his head as though to clear it.

'Oh, hullo, Avy, old girl,' he said. 'I was having a nightmare. Didn't know you were here.'

'I'm not the only one who's here,' said Aviatrix. 'Look on your other side.'

Obediently Clawed turned his huge head, to see a very small head close by.

'Hullo, Daddy,' said Nosy.

'Daddy?' said Clawed. 'What are you talking about, boy? What's he mean, Avy?'

'This is our son, dear,' said Aviatrix proudly. 'Our firstborn. Only hatched this morning, but already he's a good flier.'

'Because I'm nidifugous, Daddy,' said Nosy.

Clawed shook his head in puzzlement.

'Sounds like one of those long words your mother uses,' he said. 'Half the time I never understand what she's on about.'

'You never were very bright, dear,' said Aviatrix, 'but I think our son is an infant prodigy.'

'What does "infant prodigy" mean, Mum?' asked Nosy.

'A highly intelligent child,' replied his mother.

Nosy felt very pleased at this. He couldn't kick his little legs because he was hanging by them, but he flapped his little wings instead.

'Don't suppose he even knows what he is,' said Clawed grumpily. 'What are you, boy, eh?'

'I'm a pterodactyl, Daddy,' said Nosy. 'Like you. Though I don't suppose I'll ever be as big as you.'

Or as silly, said Aviatrix to herself, fond as I am of him.

'What's your name, boy?' asked

Clawed. 'If I know your mother, she'll have given you a very long one.'

'No, Daddy,' said Nosy. 'I'm just Nosy.'

'Are you indeed?' said Clawed. 'Poking your snout into other people's business, eh? Well, ask me no questions and I'll tell you no lies.'

'No, I mean, my name is Nosy.'

'Oh,' said Clawed. 'Oh, I see. By the way, my name's Clawed.'

'I know,' said Nosy, 'but I can't call you that. You're my father.'

Clawed hung in silence for a while, deep in thought. Then he said 'You're right, my son. You'd better stick to "Daddy". Take him away now, Avy. I haven't had enough sleep,' and he closed his eyes.

'Come on, then, Nosy,' said his mother.
'Daddy's tired,' and she dropped from the
branch and spread her wings and flew off.

Nosy followed.

'Where are we going now, Mum?' he
asked.

'To get some breakfast.'

'What sort of breakfast?'

'Bugs.'

'What does that mean?'

'Flies and beetles and gnats and midges and things. We are carnivores, you see.'

'What does that mean?'

'We eat meat, including insects. There should be lots flying about on a nice warm morning like this. Specially if there should be a dead dinosaur lying about somewhere. There'll be masses of flies around it,' said Aviatrix.

Before long she said, 'We're in luck, Nosy. Look down there.'

Nosy looked down and on the ground below he saw a simply enormous body, with clouds of flies buzzing upon and around it.

'Whatever is that, Mum?' he asked.

'Brachiosaurus.'

'But it's so huge! Whatever could have killed it?'

'T. rex, I expect.'

'T. rex? That's what Daddy shouted out in his nightmare. What does it mean, Mum?'

'Tyrannosaurus rex,' said his mother. 'The fiercest, fastest flesh-eating dinosaur of all. A truly nightmarish creature.'

'What does it look like, Mum?' asked Nosy.

'Oh, stop your everlasting questions, Nosy, do! Tuck in to these flies,' said Aviatrix.

She swooped down upon the swarm of insects hovering above the dead brachiosaurus and snapped up the largest. Nosy, copying, began to catch the smallest.

Then his mother dropped down and landed upon the enormous dinosaur. Nosy followed her. All kinds of delicious little creatures were crawling over the brachiosaurus.

Nosy said, 'But, Mum, what does T. rex look like?'

'Well,' said Aviatrix, with her mouth full, 'it's got a massive body and a short, thick neck and a large head and a battery of long, sharp teeth. It has tiny forelegs but very big muscular back legs on which it stands upright.'

'Oh,' said Nosy. 'Mum?'

'What now?'

'There's one coming.'

Chapter Three

A terrifying roar split the air. Aviatrix looked up from her meal of fat flies.

'So there is,' she said.

'Mum,' said Nosy, 'hadn't we better push off before it arrives?'

Every time T. rex roared, Nosy could see those long, sharp teeth, and they looked very sharp indeed.

'No hurry,' said Aviatrix. 'Time for a bit of fun. Do you remember what my name means?'

'Yes, Mum. Female flier.'

'And what else did I tell you?'

'You said you were paramount among all pterodactyls in the skills of flying.'

'Quite right, Nosy. Watch this,' said Aviatrix, and she took off and flew directly at the approaching tyrannosaurus.

Seeing her coming, it reared up to its full height and opened wide that huge mouth crammed with sharp teeth. It thought this was going to be an easy meal.

Now Aviatrix showed just how skilled a flier she was. As she neared that open mouth, she suddenly shot straight up into the air. And, as she zoomed over the head

of T. rex, she sank her sharp claws into its snout.

T. rex let out a loud bellow, not of pain (for its skin was too thick to be much harmed by a scratch from a pterodactyl) but of rage at the cheek of the creature. It watched in fury as Aviatrix now put on a show of aerobatics.

First she looped the loop, high above the great flesh-eater, then she dived back down, straight at it, so that the watching Nosy felt sure that his mother's last moment had come.

But no, gracefully she side-slipped past the open mouth and then began to sweep round and round T. rex's neck in tight circles, while it snapped furiously at her. It rocked unsteadily on its hind feet, becoming quite giddy in its vain efforts to catch this pest.

Shooting skywards once more in the steepest of climbs, Aviatrix hovered for a moment high above the tyrannosaurus. Then, folding her leathery wings, she dropped, twisting and turning like a falling leaf, apparently totally out of control.

It looked to Nosy as though his mother was going to go straight down the throat of T. rex. But all its last snap at her earned it was a mouthful of fresh air and another scratch on the nose.

Once more Aviatrix slipped past those gaping jaws and then climbed high, to perform one last magnificent feat of aerobatics. She spread her wings wide and rolled, with first her right wing pointing skywards, then her left, over and over and over, before she finally flew back to the body of the brachiosaurus, towards which the raging T. rex was now rushing at top speed.

'Scramble, Nosy!' she called down. 'I think our friend is a bit upset.'

'Gosh, Mum, you really are a paramount

flier!' said Nosy as they flew away together.
'What was that last thing you did?'

'That,' said his mother, 'was the
Victory Roll.'

When Clawed eventually woke up, he
remembered that something nice had
happened. What was it? Oh yes, he was

a father, he had a son, Avy had brought
the boy along to see him. What was he
called? Oh yes, Nosy, that was it.

Clever little chap too, thought Clawed,
knows some long words already, just like
his mother. I don't know any long words.
Oh no, wait a minute, I do know some.
Pterodactyl to begin with, and – let's see
now – diplodocus and iguanodon and
allosaurus and stegosaurus and triceratops.

Not bad, eh? What have I left out? Oh, I know, horrible old Tyrannosaurus rex. Had a nightmare about it, didn't I? Sooner call it T. rex, though – short names are easier. Could shorten the others, I suppose. Dip. Ig. Al. Steg. Tri. No, it doesn't quite work.

Clawed yawned, tired by so much thinking. He was about to doze off again when he heard two voices.

'Clawed!' said one, and, 'Daddy!' said the other, and the branch creaked as his wife and his son landed to hang upside down on either side of him.

'Hullo,' he said. 'Where have you two been?'

'Nosy will tell you,' replied Aviatrix.

'Oh, Daddy!' cried Nosy. 'We've had

ever such an exciting time! We were
feeding on a brachiosaurus –'

'What, eating it?' interrupted Clawed.
'How did you manage that?'

'Don't be silly, Clawed,' said Aviatrix.
'Nosy means we were on a brachiosaurus,
feeding. On flies. Don't interrupt the boy.'

'Oh, sorry,' said Clawed. 'Go on, Nosy.'

'And then,' went on Nosy, 'what d'you
think we saw, Daddy?'

'Haven't a clue,' said Clawed.

'Have a guess.'

'One of our relations, perhaps? Haven't
seen my brother for a while. You'd like
your Uncle Eggbert, Nosy. He's nearly as
big as me.'

And nearly as silly, said Aviatrix to
herself, smiling fondly at her husband.

'No, Daddy,' said Nosy. 'It wasn't a pterosaur we saw, it was a dinosaur.'

Dip? Ig? Al? Steg? Tri? thought Clawed. I don't know.

'I give up,' he said.

'We saw a T. rex!' said Nosy. 'And Mum did some absolutely fantastic, superlative aerobatics.'

'Which you will probably be able to do just as well when you're grown up, Nosy,' said Aviatrix. 'Thanks to your primogeniture.'

'What does that word mean, Avy?' asked Clawed.

'Literally,' replied Aviatrix, 'it means the circumstance of being firstborn. If you comprehend the purport of my prognostication.'

Clawed looked blank.

'Mum means I'm going to be a good flier, Daddy,' said Nosy.

Clawed looked pleased.

'You're bound to be, my son,' he said, 'with a father like me.'

Chapter Four

Aviatrix looked at her large husband with a mixture of amusement and pride. He may be silly, she thought, but he is a good flier. Not as good as me, of course, but faster, I have to admit. With that enormous wingspan of his and his great strength, I reckon he could beat any pterodactyl on earth in a race. I bet Nosy

would be surprised. Shall I get old
Clawed to show off his speed? Why not!

'Let's get airborne, Clawed,' she said to
her husband, 'and then you'll be able to
see how well Nosy is doing. Anyway,
you need some exercise. You're always
hanging about.'

Clawed looked doubtful.

'Come on, Daddy,' said Nosy. 'I'd love
to fly with you. Mum is a bit too fast for
me.' But you won't be, he thought. You're
too big and heavy and lazy.

Clawed yawned.

'Oh, all right,' he said. 'If I must, I
must,' and he unclasped his huge claws
and dropped down till he was clear of all
the branches of the tree. Then he glided
out into the open, where the others

joined him, and the three of them set off in line, Nosy in the middle, one parent on either side of him.

'Mum! Daddy! Where are we going?' he asked.

'Let's go to the lake,' said Clawed. 'I'm thirsty.'

'All right,' said Aviatrix, 'and then we can go on to the Great Plain. Now then, Nosy, we'll give you a start. Show Daddy how fast you can fly.'

Nosy beat his little wings as hard as he could and pulled away ahead of his parents.

'Good boy!' he heard them shout, and then came the flap of much much larger wings as Aviatrix caught him up and passed him. A moment later Clawed came thundering by. His wings, Nosy could see, were even bigger, much much bigger, and although he beat them more slowly, they carried him along at such a rate that he in turn caught up with Aviatrix and swept past her.

Gosh! He's fast! He must be the fastest pterodactyl in the world, thought Nosy.

In front of and below him now, he could see a great sheet of water. His parents were gliding down towards it. First his father and then his mother skimmed the surface of the lake, wings splayed wide, mouths wide open. They drank as they flew, and Nosy copied as best he could.

At the far side of the lake were trees that hung out over the water. The family settled there, to hang upside down on a convenient branch.

Nosy shook himself.

'I'm wet, Mum,' he said.

'You have to learn the trick of it,' said Aviatrix, 'but you did well.'

'And you flew well, my boy,' said Clawed.

'Gosh! You're fast, Daddy!' said Nosy.

Clawed looked pleased.

'You must be the fastest pterodactyl in the world,' said Nosy.

Clawed looked very pleased.

'He is,' said Aviatrix.

'Oh, I don't know,' said Clawed.

'Yes, you are,' said Aviatrix. 'Don't argue. Now then, let's go on to the Great Plain.'

'But, Mum,' said Nosy, 'I'm tired. Can't we rest for a bit?'

'Good idea,' said Clawed.

'No,' said Aviatrix. 'But I'll tell you what. You can have a piggyback.'

'What does that mean, Mum?' asked Nosy.

'You can have a ride on Daddy's back. That'll give you a good rest.'

'Can I really?'

'Of course you can.'

'But, Avy,' said Clawed, 'I wouldn't mind a rest too.'

'Nonsense,' said Aviatrix. 'Jump on now, Nosy. Oops-a-daisy!'

Nosy never forgot the thrill he felt when, clinging tightly to his father's back, he looked down and saw the Great Plain for the first time.

In the land where the pterodactyls lived there were three different kinds of country.

Firstly, there was the dry stony desert, where Nosy had hatched. Here, each female would lay her solitary egg among the hot rocks.

Secondly, there were the woods, full of convenient trees for pterodactyls to hang upon.

And thirdly, there was the Great Plain: miles and miles of grassland, where all the great plant-eating dinosaurs lived.

Now, as Nosy looked down in wonder, he saw herds of huge creatures such as diplodocuses and ankylosauruses and stegosauruses.

Nosy's parents dropped lower and hovered above a single enormous dinosaur that was moving very slowly, grazing on the coarse grasses.

'Gosh! What's that, Daddy?' he cried.

'Apatosaurus,' said Clawed.

'It's so *big*!' cried Nosy. 'They're all so big, all these beasts below us!'

'Second-class creatures, the lot of them,' said his mother scornfully.

'Not a patch on us,' said his father proudly.

'Why not?'

'Because,' said his parents with one voice, 'they can't fly!'

At that moment something came out from beneath the giant dinosaur. Something which had been sheltering there and had been alarmed by the flying creatures overhead.

It was a baby apatosaurus.

Chapter Five

'Ma,' said the baby apatosaurus, 'what were those funny things in the sky?'

'Pterodactyls,' replied her mother, whose name was Gargantua.

'I was frightened,' said the baby.

'No need,' said Gargantua. 'Pterodactyls are fourth-rate creatures, much inferior to us.'

'Why?'

'They've only got two legs. They can't walk about like we dinosaurs can. Just remember that of all creatures dinosaurs are the best and that of all dinosaurs apatosauruses are the greatest.'

'Yes, Ma,' said the baby.

'One day,' said Gargantua, 'you'll grow up to be a big girl, a very big girl, as big as me.'

'And then I won't be frightened of anything, Ma?'

Gargantua looked down at her small daughter.

'Certainly not,' she said.

No point in worrying her, she thought. With a bit of luck she may never meet a T. rex.

Just then another apatosaurus, even bigger than Gargantua, plodded heavily towards them.

'Oh, look!' said Gargantua. 'Here comes your father,' and she called, 'Titanic!'

'What does that mean, Ma?' asked the baby.

'It's his name, dear,' replied Gargantua.

'Which reminds me, you haven't got a name yet. I can't go on calling you "baby".'

She waited until her huge husband reached them and then asked, 'What shall we call her?'

'Call who?' asked Titanic.

'This baby of ours. Your daughter.'

'Didn't know I had one,' said Titanic.

'Well, now you do. Say hullo to your father, baby.'

'Hullo, Pa,' said the little apatosaurus.

'Hullo, Wotsyername,' said Titanic. 'What's she called, Gargy?'

'She hasn't got a name yet. Can you think of one?'

'She's very small,' said Titanic.

'She's very young,' said Gargantua.

'She'll be big one day.'

'Suppose so,' said Titanic. 'But just now she looks a bantamweight. Tell you what, Gargy, let's call her Banty.'

Gargantua turned to her daughter.

'How about that, baby?' she said. 'Shall we call you Banty? How would you like that?'

'I don't mind,' said the little apatosaurus.

She looked up at her enormous parents. Shall I really be as big as them one day, she thought? Shall I have four great legs like pillars and a very long tail and a very very long neck?

She looked carefully at their heads.

'Why are your nostrils so high up?' she asked.

'So that we can stand in very deep water, almost completely submerged, and yet still be able to breathe,' said her mother.

'But why would you want to stand in very deep water?'

'To get cool,' replied her father.

And to escape from a T. rex, he thought, but no point in worrying the child with that. With a bit of luck she may never meet one.

'Talking of which,' he went on, 'I could do with a dip. I'm hot and I'm hungry. I could murder a good meal of waterweed.'

So they plodded off towards the lake, where Banty stood in the shallows, watching as Titanic and Gargantua plunged their long necks deep under the water to pull up great mouthfuls of weed.

She looked up into the sky, remembering the flying creatures she had seen. I wonder why Ma was so nasty about pterodactyls, she said to herself. I thought they were interesting, specially the little one. It was rather sweet.

Meanwhile Nosy and Clawed and Aviatrix had arrived back at their perch in the woods. Upside down, Nosy looked at the ground below, remembering the apatosaurus and its baby. It was rather sweet, he thought. Wonder why Mum and

Daddy were so nasty about apatosauruses.
I thought they were interesting. I'd like
to meet that little one again.

Early next morning, while his parents
were still asleep, Nosy dropped off the
branch and flew away in the direction of
the Great Plain. Which is beyond the lake,
he said to himself, and I can't miss that.

Sure enough, before long he saw beneath
him the great sheet of water. Round its
edges a number of dinosaurs were
drinking – diplodocuses, ankylosauruses,
stegosauruses and many others – but Nosy
could not see the apatosaurus family.

This was not surprising, since all that
was showing of them were, in deep
water, the nostrils of Gargantua and

Titanic, and in the shallows, where she
was practising going underwater, the very
small nostrils of their child.

By a lucky chance, Banty popped her
head up as the young pterodactyl was
flapping by.

That's it, thought Nosy, that's the one,
I'm sure, and he dropped lower and
called out, 'Good morning!'

Banty waded out of the water and stood looking up at him.

'Good morning,' she said. 'You're a pterodactyl, aren't you?'

'Yes,' replied Nosy. 'And you're an apatosaurus. Excuse me asking, but what's your name?'

'Banty. What's yours?'

'Nosy.'

'Oh. Are you a girl or a boy?'

'Boy. And you?'

'Girl.'

'It's strange,' said Nosy, 'but my mum and daddy are very rude about apatosauruses.'

'Why?'

'Because you can't fly.'

'Oh,' said Banty. 'Well, funnily enough

my ma and pa are very rude about pterodactyls.'

'Why?'

'Because you've only got two legs, so you can't walk.'

'But I don't want to walk,' said Nosy. 'Flying's nicer.'

'And I don't want to fly,' said Banty. 'Walking's nicer.'

They looked at one another with interest.

'Talking's nice too,' said Nosy.

'Yes, it is,' said Banty, 'but it must be tiring for you to keep flapping about, Nosy, while I'm standing comfortably.'

'No problem, Banty,' said Nosy. 'If you'll just walk over to this tree that overhangs the water,' and he grasped a convenient branch with his little claws and swung over to hang upside down.

'Wow! That's cute!' said Banty, and she stretched up her little neck and pulled a bunch of leaves off the branch.

'Gosh! That's clever!' said Nosy. 'You must be a herbivore.'

'What's that mean?' asked Banty.

'A creature that eats grass and leaves. Me, I'm a carnivore.'

'Where did you learn long words like those?'

'From my mum. She knows lots of long words. She's clever, my mum.'

'So's my ma,' said Banty.

'What about your father?' asked Nosy.

'He's not all that bright.'

'Nor's my daddy. Perhaps females are always cleverer than males. What do you think?'

'I don't think that's true,' said Banty. 'It's obvious to me that you are a much brighter dinosaur than I am.'

'Well, actually,' said Nosy, 'I'm not strictly a dinosaur. I'm a pterosaur. "*Pteron*" means a wing and "*saurus*" means a lizard.'

'Oh. Well, what does the "*dino*" bit of dinosaur mean?'

'Huge and terrible.'

'Wow! I like it!' said Banty.

She looked round at the sound of a mighty splashing in the lake.

'Here come Ma and Pa,' she said. 'You better beat it, Nosy, before they start being rude about you. But come back another day, won't you?'

'I will,' said Nosy as he dropped off his branch.

'See you, my friend!' he squeaked as he flew away.

Chapter Six

Gargantua and Titanic came lumbering up towards their daughter. They were dripping wet, and covered in mud and waterweed.

'Whatever was that you were talking to, Banty?' her mother asked.

'A pterodactyl, Ma. A young one. He's nice.'

'Nice!' said Gargantua. 'I'm surprised

at you, speaking to such a creature. You don't know where it's been.'

'Dirty things they are,' rumbled Titanic.

'Nosy isn't dirty, Pa,' said Banty.

'Oh,' said Gargantua, 'so we're on first-name terms already, are we?'

'He can hang upside down, Ma,' said Banty.

'Hang upside down!' said her mother in

tones of horror. 'Well, there you are! How can it possibly keep clean?'

'What d'you mean, Ma?'

'Well, goodness me, Banty, you're old enough now to know that all creatures have to . . . um, er . . . make themselves comfortable. No one can digest everything that is eaten. Some of it is, er, wasted. It has to be got rid of.'

'What d'you mean, Ma?'

'Droppings,' said Titanic heavily. 'We all do 'em.'

'But,' said Gargantua, 'we do them on the grass.'

'Or in the water,' said Titanic.

'But just imagine,' said Gargantua, 'a creature that is hanging upside down and suddenly needs to do its, er . . .'

'. . . droppings,' said Titanic.

'. . . and you can easily realize that it is going to make itself filthy. I very much hope, Banty, that you will have nothing more to do with it.'

Nosy's a 'he', not an 'it', thought Banty, and we're friends, and if I want to see him again, I *shall*, Ma, so there.

Meanwhile, back in the woods, Aviatrix and Clawed were waking up to find that Nosy was absent.

'Where's he gone?' said his mother.

'Don't know,' said his father.

'What are we going to do?'

'Don't know.'

'Wherever he's gone, he'll come back, won't he?'

Clawed, hanging by his huge talons, stretched his huge wings and yawned a huge yawn.

'Don't know,' he replied.

You don't know anything, thought Aviatrix angrily, but before she could say more Nosy came flying in at speed.

In one fluent movement he turned on his back, reached up with his little legs,

caught the branch with his little claws
and hung there, swinging to and fro.

Aviatrix turned her anger on her son.

'Wherever have you been, you naughty
boy?' she cried.

'To the lake, Mum.'

'To the lake? Whatever for?'

'A drink, I expect,' said Clawed.
'That's why I go there. I like a drink,
now and again.'

'No, Daddy,' said Nosy. 'I went to meet
a friend.'

'A friend?' said his mother. 'Another
pterodactyl, you mean?'

'No, Mum.'

'What, then?'

'A young apatosaurus. The one we saw
yesterday. On the Great Plain. She's

called Banty. She's nice.'

'Well!' said Aviatrix. 'I'm dumbfounded!'

'What's that mean, Mum?'

'Reduced to silence.'

'But you're talking.'

'Hold your tongue, child. I am utterly flabbergasted.'

'What's that mean?'

'Oh, stop your endless questions. I cannot tell you how surprised I am that you should be speaking to such a creature.'

'But you are telling me, Mum,' said Nosy.

'You don't know where it's been,' said Clawed. 'They're dirty things, they are.'

He did a huge poo, which, by a stroke of luck, missed his head and fell to the ground below.

'They're not dirty, Daddy,' said Nosy.

'They come off the Great Plain and go and bathe in the lake. Banty certainly isn't dirty.'

'Banty!' said Aviatrix. 'What a silly name for a silly flightless creature. I trust you'll have nothing more to do with it.'

Banty's a 'she', not an 'it', thought Nosy. She's my friend and I hope I'm hers, and I *shall* see her again, Mum, so there.

Chapter Seven

Of all the creatures that lived on the Great Plain, the nastiest was Tyrannosaurus rex, and of all tyrannosauruses the biggest and most bloodthirsty was the one that Aviatrix and Nosy had met when they were fly-catching on the body of the dead brachiosaurus. His name was Hack the Ripper.

What he liked best was to hunt a dinosaur – any one of the many kinds of grass-eaters that roamed the plain – and kill it, and eat it, or as much of it as he could stomach. Hack's favourite prey was baby dinosaur, not because it was too slow to escape him – they were all too slow, whatever their age – but because a baby made such a lovely meal: so tender, so tasty, so mouth-watering.

On one particular morning he was walking upright across the plain, scanning the various herds of animals with his cold, hard eyes, looking to see if there was a nice fat baby nearby.

As soon as they saw him, diplodocuses, iguanodons and the rest all moved away, slowly of course, turning small heads on

the end of long necks to see if he was
following.

Hack the Ripper was hungry, but not
ravenously hungry. He decided he would
have a drink – it was a hot day – before
beginning his hunting.

It so happened that Titanic and
Gargantua were standing at the edge of
the lake, at the very spot indeed to which
Hack was heading.

They had been out grazing on the plain
since first light and their huge stomachs
were packed full of grass. Now, when
they saw T. rex approaching, they
splashed as hastily as they could out into
deep water and submerged. Only their
nostrils showed.

Some minutes passed, and then, slowly, Titanic put his head up and then so did Gargantua.

'It's all right, Gargy,' said Titanic. 'The brute is going,' and they watched as Hack strode away back to the grasslands.

'Horrible thing!' said Gargantua. 'I wonder what wretched animal will die today to feed its disgusting appetite?'

'They say it likes baby dinosaurs best,' said Titanic.

The two great apatosauruses stretched up their long necks and stared, first at one another and then, as the same thought struck them, all around the lake and its shore, and with one voice, a horrified voice, they cried, 'Where's our Banty?'

Chapter Eight

Thinking about his new friend, Nosy had become worried about her. He knew all about T. rex – he'd seen one, close up, after all – but he was pretty sure that Banty did not.

Obviously her parents had never told her, never warned her of the danger of the plain's fiercest flesh-eater. They just hope, he supposed, that she'll never meet one.

She should be told, he thought. I'll get Mum and Daddy to tell her, and I might even be able to persuade them to fly over and have a chat with Banty's ma and pa.

With all this in mind, he had flown off very early that morning in search of his friend. By luck, he found her at the lake's edge. He glided down.

'Hullo, Banty!' he called.

Banty looked up.

'Oh, hullo, Nosy!' she cried. 'Where are you off to?'

'I've just come to see you,' Nosy said. 'I wanted to ask you something.'

'What?'

'Well, how would you like to come and

67

see where I live with my mum and my
daddy?'

'Where's that?'

'In the woods. It's not far. You wouldn't
be scared, would you?'

'Scared?' said Banty. 'Of what?'

'Oh, of . . . um . . . leaving your ma
and pa for a while.'

'No,' said Banty. 'They probably won't
even notice I'm gone.'

'Well, come on, then,' said Nosy. 'I'll
fly very slowly above to show you the way.'

And to keep a good lookout for
You-Know-Who, he thought.

Before long, Banty was standing in the
pterodactyls' wood, looking up at Clawed
and Aviatrix as they hung, still asleep,

above her. They were on a fresh branch
because, the previous evening, Nosy had
persuaded his parents to move. He didn't
want Banty to have to stand in a bed of
deep, pongy poo.

'Mum, Daddy, wake up!' he called,
hitching on to the branch beside them.
'I've brought my friend Banty to meet you.'

Aviatrix opened her eyes and looked down in horror at the baby apatosaurus. The shock rendered her speechless.

'Good morning, Nosy's mum,' said Banty in the politest of tones. 'I'm very pleased to meet you. Nosy thought I might like to see the wood where you live. It's beautiful, isn't it?'

'It's pulchritudinous,' said Nosy.

'Nosy tells me,' said Banty, 'that you have taught him a great many long words. You must be very clever.'

'Sagacious,' said Nosy.

'That too,' said Banty.

'The epithets are synonymous,' said Aviatrix.

Quite a nice little thing, she thought. Well, not little, but nice. Good manners.

At this point Clawed woke up. He was about to do a poo, always his first act of the day, but seeing what stood below him, he refrained.

'Who's this?' he said.

'My friend, Daddy,' said Nosy.

'Good morning, sir,' said Banty.

Clawed was so astonished at being addressed with such respect that he almost fell off the branch.

'Morning,' he said.

'Her name is Banty, Daddy,' said Nosy, 'and I've brought her to see you and Mum for a very special reason. Knowing how clever you both are.'

Aviatrix looked very pleased at this, Clawed very puzzled.

'And what is this very special reason?' asked Aviatrix.

'I want you to warn her,' said Nosy.

'Warn her? Against what?'

'T. rex.'

'What's that?' asked Banty.

'Tyrannosaurus rex,' replied Aviatrix. 'The fiercest of the carnivores.'

'Please, Nosy's mum — what is a carnivore?'

'A meat-eater. And stop calling me

"Nosy's mum". My name is Aviatrix.'

'And mine's Clawed,' said Clawed, 'but you can go on calling me "sir" if you like – I quite fancy it.'

'Hang on a minute,' said Nosy.

'We all are,' said Clawed, taking a fresh grip on the branch with his large talons.

'No, Daddy, I mean, let me tell you what's worrying me. You can see that Banty's parents have never told her about T. rex, though I don't know why. Which means she's in terrible danger if she ever comes across one.'

'She is vulnerable,' said Aviatrix.

'What's that mean, Avy?' asked Clawed.

'Capable of being physically wounded or injured or, in Banty's case, killed and eaten.'

Banty shuddered (and when an

apatosaurus, even a small one, shudders,
it's quite a sight).

'What does this awful thing look like?'
she said, and the two adult pterodactyls
told her, each in its own way.

Aviatrix's description was full of long
words like 'formidable', 'terroristic',
'repulsive' and 'unprepossessing'.

Clawed, who understood none of these adjectives, simply said, 'Big and scary.'

'But surely, sir,' said Banty, 'this T. rex creature couldn't kill something as big as an apatosaurus?'

'Easily,' said Clawed.

'And you're only a baby one,' said Aviatrix.

By now she had warmed to this odd-looking, innocent young animal.

'You must take great care, Banty, dear,' she said. 'We can always escape by flying, but you can't.'

'Mum, Daddy,' said Nosy, 'please could you do my friend here a big favour?'

'Indubitably,' said his mother, 'and before you ask me, Clawed, that means without a doubt.'

'What d'you want?' asked Clawed.

'Could you both come over to the lake with me so that you can meet Banty's parents? Neither of us knows why, but they don't seem to like pterodactyls and you don't like apatosauruses. Banty and I are friends, but wouldn't it be nice if we were all friends – both families, I mean?'

'Would you like us to come, Banty?' Nosy's mother asked.

'Oh yes, I would, please!'

'Then we will,' said Clawed. 'I could do with a drink anyway.'

Chapter Nine

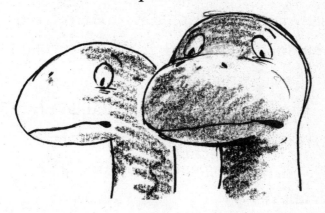

'Banty! Banty!' called Gargantua and Titanic as they lumbered round the rim of the lake, but there was no response.

When they stopped to get their breath, at a point that chanced to be the nearest to the distant woods, Gargantua gasped, 'It couldn't have taken her, could it?'

Titanic looked puzzled.

'What couldn't have taken who?' he asked.

'That T. rex we've just seen, you fool,' said Gargantua. 'Could it have taken our Banty?'

Titanic considered.

'Don't think so,' he said. 'It didn't have anything in its mouth and we weren't submerged long enough for it to have time to –'

'Stop!' cried Gargantua. 'Don't say it!' and she shuddered the most enormous apatosaurian shudder.

Just then they saw, flying towards them from the direction of the woods, three pterodactyls. There was a little one, a big one and a very big one.

'We could ask those wotchermecallits if they've seen her,' Titanic said.

'Pterodactyls!' said Gargantua scornfully. 'They wouldn't know the difference between an iguanodon and a triceratops. Stupid things! I've no use for them.'

At that moment the small pterodactyl detached itself from the two much larger ones, which were flying very slowly, and flew, very quickly, towards the apatosauruses.

'Ugh!' said Gargantua. 'One of them is coming straight to us. If it speaks, don't answer, Titanic.'

'Good morning!' squeaked Nosy when he reached them. 'I've a favour to ask you. Could I introduce my mum and my daddy to you?' There was no answer.

'Oh,' said Nosy, 'we've got Banty with us,' he added.

'What?' bellowed both apatosauruses.

'We've got Banty. We've brought her home,' said Nosy. 'Look, you can see her now.'

Titanic and Gargantua stretched up their long necks to the fullest extent, and there was their missing daughter, coming towards them, escorted by the two big pterodactyls, which were flying, very slowly, above her.

'Oh, my Banty!' called Gargantua, waddling forward. 'You're safe!'

'Ma thought you might have been eaten by that T. rex,' said Titanic.

'Oh, you saved her!' cried Gargantua to Aviatrix and Clawed. 'You saved my Banty! Oh, how can we ever thank you enough?'

Clawed looked extremely puzzled.

'Saved her?' he began, but Aviatrix quickly interrupted him.

'We are glad to have been of help,' she said to Gargantua. 'We weren't sure if Banty was aware of certain dangers.'

'Like T. rex,' said Clawed. 'Although actually . . .'

'Be quiet a minute, Clawed,' said

Aviatrix, and, 'Hang on, Daddy,' said
Nosy, a suggestion which his father
instantly obeyed, on a branch of the
nearest tree.

Aviatrix and Nosy, hovering above,
looked down at Banty, and she looked up
at them, and each knew exactly what the
others were thinking.

Let my ma and pa believe that the
pterodactyl family *did* rescue me

somehow, thought Banty, just as Aviatrix and Nosy thought, let's pretend we did rescue her. That way they'll be very grateful and we'll all be the best of friends.

When the apatosauruses had finished nuzzling the child they thought they had lost, Gargantua started to make a specch.

'First of all,' she said to Aviatrix and Nosy, 'please do join your, er . . .'

'Husband,' said Aviatrix.

'Daddy,' said Nosy.

'. . . on that branch. So much less tiring than having to beat your wings all the time,' and when they took her advice, she went on to address the three of them.

'I cannot begin to tell you,' she said, 'how grateful Titanic . . .'

'Your husband?' said Aviatrix.

'My daddy,' said Banty.

'. . . how grateful we are to all of you for saving our beloved child. We have met dear little Nosy before and now are honoured to be introduced to his parents, though I fear I do not know your names.'

'Aviatrix,' said Nosy's mother.

'Clawed,' said his father.

'I,' said Banty's mother, 'am Gargantua, and my husband, Titanic, and we are the happiest apatosauruses in the world thanks to your pterodactylic heroism in rescuing our Banty from the clutches of T. rex.'

'But –' said Clawed.

'Hang on, dear,' said Aviatrix.

'I am hanging on.'

'If you will allow me to say so,' went on

Aviatrix, 'I think that perhaps you, as Banty's parents, should have made her more aware of the danger posed by a certain carnivore . . .'

'T. rex,' said Clawed.

'. . . danger,' continued Aviatrix, 'of which she may have known nothing.'

'We should! We should!' cried Gargantua. 'Just think, Titanic, she might have become the prey of that T. rex that came to the lake if this brave pterodactyl family had not somehow rescued her. Oh, how grateful we are to you all!'

Clawed, as so often, looked puzzled.

'We rescued her, did we, Avy?' he asked.

'Of course we did!' said Aviatrix and Nosy.

Now Titanic cleared his very long throat.

'As head of the family,' he said to
Clawed, 'I must thank you, sir, from the
bottom of my heart.'

Clawed had by now realized that, what
with one thing and another, he had not
yet performed what was usually his first
act of the day, and in some confusion at
this thought and at once again being

addressed as 'sir', he became muddled and replied, 'It is I who must thank you, from the heart of my bottom.'

Then he spread his huge wings and flew hastily away to a branch on another tree, where he did his morning poo out of sight of the rest.

Chapter Ten

That first meeting, with all its misunderstanding of Banty's 'rescue', did indeed lead to friendship between the two families of dinosaurs and pterosaurs.

The mothers in particular became great friends. They would now meet regularly by the lake or on the near part of the Great Plain. Obviously this was simpler,

for the pterodactyls could fly to these
meetings. The adult apatosauruses would
have had great difficulty in making their
way into the woods. Trees would be
falling everywhere before the impact of
their bulk.

'It will be so much easier for you,
Gargantua,' said Aviatrix. 'It's not the
least trouble for us to fly to the lake or
the Great Plain or wherever we want to

meet. We are, after all, aeronauts of remarkable facility and versatility.'

'How I admire the way you have with words, Aviatrix,' said Gargantua. 'It is such a pleasure to talk with you. And you are all such good fliers.'

I just said that, thought Aviatrix. Ah well, maybe I can improve her vocabulary. Which, to some extent, she did.

Gargantua learned to say 'perambulate' instead of 'walk', 'enumerate' instead of 'count', 'cogitate' or 'deliberate' instead of 'think', and many other long words which, though familiar to Aviatrix, were quite new to the apatosaurus.

'Not the most erudite of creatures, those apatosauruses,' said Aviatrix to her husband later.

'Come again?' said Clawed.

'They don't know very much.'

'Oh,' said Clawed. 'Not as much as we do, eh?'

As I do, said Aviatrix to herself.

'She's not too bad,' she said. 'What d'you think of him?'

'Who?'

'Titanic.'

'Oh, him. Well, he's a fine figure of an apatosaurus, I must say.'

And he called me 'sir', he thought. Not a bad start.

'He's all right,' he said. 'Probably not all that clever, like we are.'

If Aviatrix had possessed eyebrows, she would have raised them.

'Perhaps you could teach him a thing or two, Clawed,' she said.

Fat chance, she thought.

Meanwhile, Banty's parents were talking about the pterodactyls.

'I must tell you, Titanic,' said Gargantua, 'that I have changed my mind about little Nosy's mother and father.'

'Have you, Gargy?' said her husband. 'Because they rescued Banty, you mean?'

'Of course. But also because they turned out to be much brighter than I thought they'd be.'

'He was?' asked Titanic.

He too would have raised his eyebrows if he'd had any.

'Well, perhaps not,' replied Gargantua,

'but she seemed quite intelligent.'

Now, when one set of parents met the other, usually by the lake, it was generally mother who talked to mother, and father to father. Because of the great difference between the two species, these conversations were always conducted in the same way. Each pterodactyl would fly to, and hang from, a branch high enough for each apatosaurus to stretch its very long neck to the fullest extent. Then each was able to speak to the other, face to face, one face of course being upside down.

The mothers talked about all kinds of different things. Their conversations were lively – and filled with long words. It was somewhat different when Clawed met Titanic.

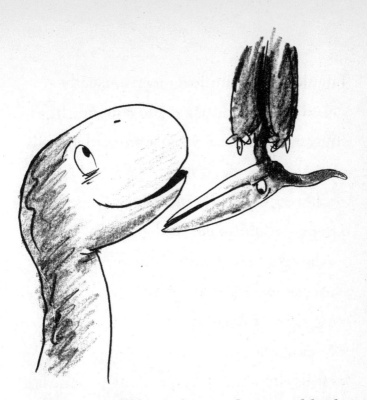

To begin with, neither male quite liked
to look the other in the eye. Their faces
may have been close, but Titanic tended
to look up into the sky or out to the
lake or over to the Great Plain, while
Clawed, partly because he was upside
down and partly because talking to

Titanic made him feel sleepy, usually stared straight down at the ground. In contrast to the conversations of their mates, theirs were short and pretty dull.

Clawed would fly in and hang up, and Titanic would make his heavy way to the tree in use and stand beneath and stretch up his long neck. A typical exchange might be as follows:

Clawed: Morning.

Titanic: Good morning, sir. I trust you're well?

C: Not too bad.

Longish pause.

C: Nice weather.

T: A trifle hot, I fear, for someone of my size. Makes walking tiring.

This last word would make Clawed yawn.

T: How fortunate you are, sir, to have the gift of flight. How pleasant it must be in the upper air.

C: Yes.

T: Your family well?

C: Yes.

Longish pause.

C: Any sign of T. rex?

T: No, I think he must be on the
   other side of the Great Plain.
C: Hope he stays there.
Short pause.
T: If you'll excuse me, sir, I'll go
   down to the lake for some
   waterweed, if I may?
C: Please do.
T plods heavily off.
C goes heavily to sleep.

These family meetings between the
pterodactyls and the apatosauruses
suited Nosy and Banty perfectly. With
their parents close by in case of trouble,
they could spend time together, chatting
and playing.

They invented some games, like

'Hide-and-Seek', where Nosy closed his eyes and counted to a hundred, while Banty went to the lake and submerged. Then, when time was up, Nosy would skim the surface of the water, searching for those two little nostrils which were all that would show of his friend.

Another game was 'Cry T. Rex!' Nosy would wait till Banty was peacefully grazing and then he'd suddenly fly hastily towards her, squeaking, 'T. rex! T. rex! Run, Banty!' and she would run (or rather waddle) as quickly as she could for the safety of the lake, while Nosy watched happily.

To pay him back for frightening her, Banty would sneak up behind a branch on which he was hanging, as quietly as

she could,
and then
suddenly cry,
'T. rex! T. rex!
Scramble, Nosy!' She
would grasp the branch in her
mouth and shake it violently as the awful
monster might have done, and then roar
with laughter as Nosy flew off in a panic.

The thought of T. rex was in everyone's
minds, but for a long time there was
mercifully no sign of Hack the Ripper.

He was hunting on the far side of the
Great Plain, where many dinosaurs had
laid their eggs some months ago. Now
there were dozens of nice fat newly
hatched babies that made easy and very
tasty meals for Hack. A river ran by this
side of the plain, so that there was no
need for the tyrannosaurus to visit the
lake for a drink.

But gradually the slow brains of
brachiosaurus or iguanodon or triceratops
took in the fact that they were losing a lot
of their babies, and that perhaps they had
better migrate across the plain.

The herds made for the lake, thinking
they would escape from Hack the Ripper.

But they were to be disappointed.

He followed.

Chapter Eleven

Both Nosy's and Banty's families noticed that there were a great many more dinosaurs about the place. Though there was as yet no sign of the Tyrannosaurus rex, they became worried that Hack might come to hunt there again.

The three pterodactyls took it upon themselves to do regular aerial surveys of that part of the Great Plain nearest to the lake. Flying up to a good height, they had a fine pterosaur's-eye view, and would be able to give warning, in time for the apatosaurus family to take cover under water, save for their nostrils.

Aviatrix then arranged a duty roster. Each morning she would fly out first, to be relieved later by Nosy, who in turn gave way to his father. (Clawed did not like early rising.)

One mid-morning, Nosy left the woods and flew off to take over from his mother. He saw no sign of her in the skies, but then caught sight of her as she skimmed low over the part-eaten body of a stegosaurus. Clouds of insects were busy about it, and she was busy about them.

She flew up when she saw Nosy approaching.

'Well,' she said, 'what d'you think killed that, my son?'

'T. rex?'

'Exactly. He's back. I haven't seen any sight of him yet, he's probably busy digesting this breakfast of his. But you keep your eyes skinned. Daddy will be along later.'

After his mother had gone, Nosy flew
up high to scan the plain below. A number
of herds of different sorts of dinosaurs
were grazing below him, but then, suddenly,
they all began to move about nervously,
and then, in a kind of mass panic, to
hurry away, to left or to right, as though
some fearful enemy was coming.

T. rex, thought Nosy?

He flew lower over the hustling herds,

and, sure enough, there, marching forward towards the lake on his two great hind legs, his tiny forelegs held against his massive chest, his jaws agape to show those long dagger-like teeth, was Hack the Ripper. He was growling, and soon his growls turned to roars.

There's nothing I can do to save any of these wretched beasts below me, thought Nosy, but I must alert Banty and her ma and pa, so that they can get into the water, and he set off towards the lake. Halfway there he saw a solitary figure, its head buried in the grass of the plain, quietly eating. It was a apatosaurus. It was a young apatosaurus. It was Banty!

Quickly he flew towards her and hovered above her.

'T. rex! T. rex! Run, Banty!' he squealed.

Banty did not even look up.

'Not now, Nosy,' she said, 'not while I'm having my lunch. Anyway, I'm a bit bored with playing "Cry T. Rex!" We'll have to think of another game to play.'

'But this isn't a game, Banty, this is real!' squeaked Nosy. 'Can't you hear him? Look, you can see him now, and he's coming straight for you!'

At this Banty raised her head, stretched her neck and saw Hack.

He was no more than ten apatosaurus-lengths away, and the lake was about the same distance from Banty. She would never reach it in time, he was so much faster on his two legs than she was on her four. At the sight of her, Hack roared even louder.

If only Mum were here, thought Nosy, she could fly at him and scratch his snout like she did before. There's only one thing for it – I'll have to try to do the same.

But at that moment he saw his father come flying from the woods, across the lake and over the fleeing apatosaurus.

'Daddy, Daddy!' he squealed. 'It's T. rex! He's going to kill Banty! Can you do something? Please!'

Clawed may have been slow-witted, but now he showed how quick he could be in action.

'Out of the way, boy!' he cried, and he dived upon the fast-approaching Hack the Ripper.

Then, spreading his great wings wide,

he hovered directly in front of the tyrannosaurus so as to obscure the creature's view of the way ahead.

Snap and snarl as he might, Hack could not shift Clawed out of his path. So he didn't see Banty reach the lake, splosh into it and submerge.

As Clawed wheeled away, Hack dashed on down to the water's edge, but there was nothing to be seen except, some way out, a small pair of nostrils. These, of course, Hack the Ripper did not notice, as he stood knee-deep, cursing the pterodactyl that had blocked his view of the prey.

'Gosh, Daddy!' said Nosy as they circled above. 'You played a blinder!'

Chapter Twelve

Hack the Ripper was furious. Roaring
and snarling, he strode back to the body
of the stegosaurus, hacking at it to stuff
himself full of meat. All the dinosaurs on
that part of the Great Plain moved as
hastily as they could out of sight of the
angry tyrannosaurus. Once again, had
they known it, they were in fact quite

safe for a while. He would not hunt till he was hungry again.

Gargantua and Titanic had been out in the lake, gathering their daily ration of waterweed, and had seen the drama of Banty's escape.

'Again!' cried Gargantua. 'Again our friends the pterodactyls have saved our Banty!'

'Old Clawed,' said Titanic, 'was pretty good, wasn't he, Gargy?'

'Magnificent,' said his wife. 'Let us collect Banty and then we will all walk to the woods to thank him.'

Later that afternoon, Nosy and his parents were hanging from a favourite branch when they heard a lot of noise in the distance. It sounded like branches breaking, which it was.

Banty could have walked among the trees without damaging them, but Titanic and Gargantua, who were much of a size – enormous – could not.

As they neared the pterodactyls' roost, Titanic attempted to make his way between two very large trees that were growing close together, too close for a apatosaurus to pass. He became stuck.

'I'm stuck, Gargy!' he called. 'What shall I do?'

'Use your brains,' Gargantua called back.

Titanic thought about this advice for a while, with no result. Then, growing annoyed, he began to lean sideways, first against one tree, then against the other, until, with a tremendous crash, first one and then the other tree fell, torn up by the roots.

Titanic walked on till he caught up with his wife and his daughter, and all three dinosaurs stood below the high branch from which the three pterosaurs were hanging.

'Aviatrix, dear,' Gargantua called up, 'we have come, Titanic and I, to thank your husband for his heroic efforts in once again saving our child. What do you say, Banty?'

'Thank you, sir,' said Banty.

'And please, sir, accept my grateful thanks,' said Titanic.

Daughter and father both calling me 'sir', thought Clawed. I wish the mother would too, but you can't have everything.

'My dear Gargantua,' said Aviatrix, 'once again we are only too glad to have been of service. Had I been on duty at the time, I should no doubt have flummoxed the dastardly curmudgeon.'

Gargantua looked pleased.

Titanic and Clawed looked puzzled.

Banty and Nosy looked at one another with amusement.

'Well,' said Gargantua, 'we must be

getting back to the lake. Why don't you all come and have a drink with us? To celebrate.'

'Shall we, Clawed?' said Aviatrix.

'Good idea, Avy,' said Clawed.

As the pterodactyls, flying very slowly above their friends, followed the path by which the apatosauruses had reached them, they noticed the two great trees that had been felled.

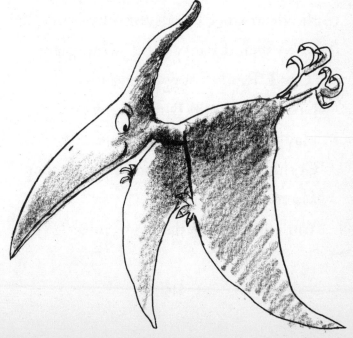

Titanic stopped and stretched up his long neck to address Clawed hovering above.

'I must apologize, sir,' he said. 'I got a bit stuck between those trees, I'm afraid.'

'Don't worry, old lad,' replied Clawed. 'Plenty more trees about.'

When they had all reached the lake and Aviatrix had flown up on a quick reconnaissance patrol to make sure the coast was clear, she and Clawed went off to the dead stegosaurus for a feast of flies. Nosy and Banty went off to play.

'"Cry T. Rex!"?' suggested Nosy.

'No, thanks,' said Banty. 'I never want to play that game again.'

'Gosh!' Nosy said. 'Your pa is so strong!'

'Ma too,' said Banty.

'You will be, one day.'

'Suppose so.'

Nosy let himself down gently on to his friend's neck. They had invented this position, which gave him a rest from flying and still allowed her, if she wished, to graze. One leg on either side of her neck meant that there was no danger of his claws scratching her.

'I've been thinking,' he said.

'Oh yes?'

'Sooner or later we've got to do something about T. rex.'

'What can we possibly do? Your mum and daddy couldn't do anything, nor could Ma and Pa.'

'True,' said Nosy. 'But you and I might, between us. There must be a way to rid us of T. rex.'

'How?'

'Give him a fright,' said Nosy. 'He's always roaring about, attacking baby dinosaurs. I bet he's really a coward. And if *we* attack *him*, he'll get the fright of his life and run away. We'll scare him off.'

Chapter Thirteen

'You must be joking,' said Banty.

'No,' said Nosy, 'I'm not. Think what we saw, just now, when we were walking or flying back through the woods.'

'What?'

'Those two great trees your pa pushed down.'

'Well?'

'Suppose,' said Nosy, 'that T. rex had been under one of those trees when it fell. That would have given him a tremendous fright – and a real bump on the head. Serve him right.'

'Wow!' said Banty. 'But how do we get him in the right place at the right time?'

'Decoy him.'

'Decoy him?'

'Yes,' said Nosy. 'Select a tree, a really big one, for your pa to push over just as T. rex goes past. He could even loosen it a bit before, to make sure it would fall. It would be a kind of trap, you see, and all we have to do is to lure the beast into it.'

'And how do we do that?' asked Banty.

'Like I say, by using a decoy, so that he's chasing it and, as he goes by the tree, your pa gives it a good push and down it comes – straight on to T. rex.'

'I see,' said Banty. 'This decoy isn't one of you, is it? He knows you could just fly away.'

'That's right.'

'And it isn't going to be Pa, who'll be waiting behind the tree. Ma too, probably.'

'That's right.'

'So,' said Banty, 'I am to be the decoy, am I, Nosy?'

'That's right.'

'Just suppose I can't go fast enough. Just suppose he catches me.'

'He won't. Mum and Daddy and I will fly in his face so he can't see where he's going. You'll be all right, Banty.'

'Thanks,' said Banty. 'Glad to know that.'

*

When they got back, they found their
parents chatting, the pterodactyls hanging
from a branch of a large lakeside tree, the
apatosauruses standing below, long necks
upstretched.

Nosy hung, Banty stood.

'Nosy has a plan,' she said to them all.

'A plan?' said Aviatrix. 'What about?'

'T. rex.'

'What are you going to do to him?' asked Gargantua.

'Frighten him,' said Nosy. 'Scare him away.'

'Don't be silly, Nosy,' said his mother. 'Run away and play. Scare T. rex indeed!'

'Hang on a minute, Avy,' said Clawed.

'I *am* hanging on!'

'Yes, but let's hear what the boy's got to say. I could do with a good laugh.'

So Nosy outlined his scheme, as he had to Banty.

'She'll have to be the decoy, of course,' he finished up.

'It's so simple, isn't it?' said Aviatrix sarcastically to the three adults. 'Titanic just drops a tree on the brute. A tree which is in the woods, which are on the other side of the lake, which means that T. rex will be chasing Banty for a long way, which means he'll catch her. I never heard of anything more injudicious.'

'What's that mean, Mum?' asked Nosy.

'Unwise.'

'I quite agree, Aviatrix,' said Gargantua. 'How perspicacious you are!'

Aviatrix looked very pleased. I only taught her that word quite recently, she thought. There's hope for her yet.

Titanic, standing looking up at the three pterodactyls on their branch, looked further up still.

'I quite agree with your good lady, sir,' he said to Clawed. 'To go all the way to your woods might not be wise. But this tree here is a very large one, which I make bold to say I could, I think, push over, especially with the assistance of my good lady. As close to the lake as we are, it seems to me that Banty could easily escape into the water.'

'No! No!' cried Gargantua. 'Forget about T. rex. We must not put our daughter's life at risk.'

'If we forget about T. rex, Gargy,' said Titanic, 'our daughter may pay for it with her life.'

There was silence for a while as they all thought about Nosy's plan, a silence broken only by a small snore as Clawed, tired by all the talk, dozed off.

'Well, Mum,' said Nosy at last, 'what do you think?'

Aviatrix looked at her son. She suddenly felt very proud of him. Fancy him thinking up such a scheme all by himself. And this was the right spot, no doubt of it, this was where T. rex came to drink, in the shade of this great tree. But wouldn't he see Titanic and Gargantua waiting behind the tree? No, because she and Clawed would pester him all the time. She would use her aerobatic skills to scratch his beastly snout, and Clawed would spread his great wings before him, to confuse him, and Nosy – could Nosy do anything when T. rex came?

'I think it is a fine plan, my son. But tell me, what will you do?' she asked.

Nosy had a sudden brainwave.

'I,' he said, 'will be the first decoy. When T. rex comes down for a drink, I'm going to flutter about on the ground in front of him, as though I were sick or had been hurt, and I'll keep doing that until he catches sight of Banty. I may not be much of a mouthful, but he won't be able

to resist chasing me. Then Banty gets into
the lake and her pa and ma fell the tree
and I'll get out of the way and it will be
"Bye-bye, T. rex." You'll see. You'll all see.'

Chapter Fourteen

The best-laid schemes often go wrong,
sometimes badly wrong, and it is rare for
a plan to succeed completely, turning
out in every detail exactly as the planner
had hoped.

But this is what happened for Nosy.

By now each member of the two families
knew exactly what to do when the time

came. They even rehearsed it, pretending that a triceratops, who happened to come down for a drink, was T. rex, and taking up their positions accordingly.

Titanic leaned on the tree quite a bit, so that it was now not as strongly rooted as it had been.

Aviatrix went out on regular long-distance patrols so as to have early warning of the approach of the tyrannosaurus.

One morning, she flew back to the lake at top speed, crying, 'Action stations!' and by the time Hack the Ripper came striding down for a drink, everyone was ready.

Clawed and Nosy took off to join Aviatrix.

Banty stood by the water's edge, looking inviting.

Titanic stood quite still behind the great tree, with Gargantua standing behind him.

Now Nosy flew down and flopped about upon the ground in front of the T. rex, who had by this time caught sight of Banty and was making for her. But he took his eye off her, thinking that he would first kill and eat this annoying flapping, flopping and seemingly flightless thing in his path.

Then Aviatrix flew in at full speed and scratched his snout, and he was blinded by rage, and by Clawed, who had spread his wide wings to spoil his view – of Banty, of Aviatrix, of Titanic and of Gargantua.

The harassed tyrannosaurus was totally bemused. He roared in rage.

'Now!' screamed Nosy at the top of his voice, and then everything happened at once, just as it was meant to.

Banty plunged into the lake, the three pterodactyls winged their way out of danger, Titanic pushed his great weight against the trunk of the tree, and Gargantua pushed her great weight against him.

With an almighty crash, the tree fell, right on top of Hack.

Then all was still, save for one small movement, the movement of something that stuck out from beneath the wreckage.

It was the tip of the tail of Hack the Ripper.

It twitched once, twice, a third time, and then it was still, forever.

Between them, the apatosauruses rolled
the tree trunk off the body of the T. rex
for all to see, as Banty came dripping out of
the lake.

'We've given him more than a fright,'
said Nosy.

'He won't hurt us any more. He's as
dead as he can be.'

'Well done, Titanic, old chap!' cried Clawed.

'I thank you too, sir,' Titanic replied.

And, 'Well done, Gargantua!' cried Aviatrix. 'Such potency!'

'There's one person,' said Banty, 'that deserves all our thanks. If it hadn't been for him, none of this would have happened.'

'Who's that, then?' asked Clawed.

'Your son, sir,' said Banty. 'My friend. Our hero. Nosy!'

Everyone looked at him and thought what a jolly fine young pterodactyl he was.

Then Titanic and Gargantua lumbered off on to the Great Plain, and Clawed and Aviatrix flew back to the woods.

'You must be tired, Nosy,' said Banty. 'Take a break.'

Gently, Nosy let himself down to sit astride his friend's neck and together they gazed reflectively at the great broken body of Hack the Ripper.

'We need never be afraid of him again,' said Banty.

'Or,' said Nosy, 'as my mum would have put it, there is no longer any necessity to regard him with trepidation.'

'But,' said Banty, 'he can't be the only T. rex in the world. Another might come, one day.'

'Not to worry, Banty,' said Nosy. 'If it does, I'll fix it. But you never know, this brute here may be the last of them. Neither Mum nor Daddy nor your ma

and pa have ever set eyes on another one.
T. rex may now be extinct.'

'What does "extinct" mean, Nosy?'
asked Banty.

Remembering exactly what his mother
had told him when he was a tiny baby,
Nosy replied, 'It means gone, finished,
kaput, dead and done for.'

'Wow!' said Banty. 'I like it!'